David Gets in Trouble

By David Shannon

Hippo

AUTHOR'S NOTE

A few years ago, my mother sent me a book I made when I was a little boy. It was illustrated with drawings of David doing all sorts of things he wasn't supposed to do, and the text consisted entirely of the words "no" and "David" – they were the only words I knew how to spell! I thought it would be fun to make a new version celebrating all the time-honoured ways mums say "no". Like the original, it was called *No, David!*

And in the sequel, *David Goes to School*, David found out that his teacher had her own ways of saying "no".

Well, now it's David's turn to speak, and it turns out that "no" is a big part of his vocabulary, too. Of course, when his mum says "no" it's because she worries about his safety, and she wants him to grow up to be a good person. Deep down, she's really saying, "I love you". But when David says "no", it usually means "I don't want to get in trouble!"

To my little troublemaker, Emma; and to Heidi, her mum, who has to say "no".

Scholastic Children's Books
Euston House, 24 Eversholt Street
London NW1 1DB, UK
a division of Scholastic Ltd
London ~ New York ~ Toronto ~ Sydney ~ Auckland
Mexico City ~ New Delhi ~ Hong Kong

First published in hardback in the USA by the Blue Sky Press, an imprint of Scholastic Inc., 2002
First published in paperback in the USA by Scholastic Inc., 2003
First published in paperback in the UK by Scholastic Ltd, 2006

Copyright © David Shannon, 2002

10 digit ISBN 0 439 95453 3
13 digit ISBN 978 0439 95453 2

2 4 6 8 10 9 7 5 3 1

When David gets in trouble,
he always says . . .

No! It's not my fault!

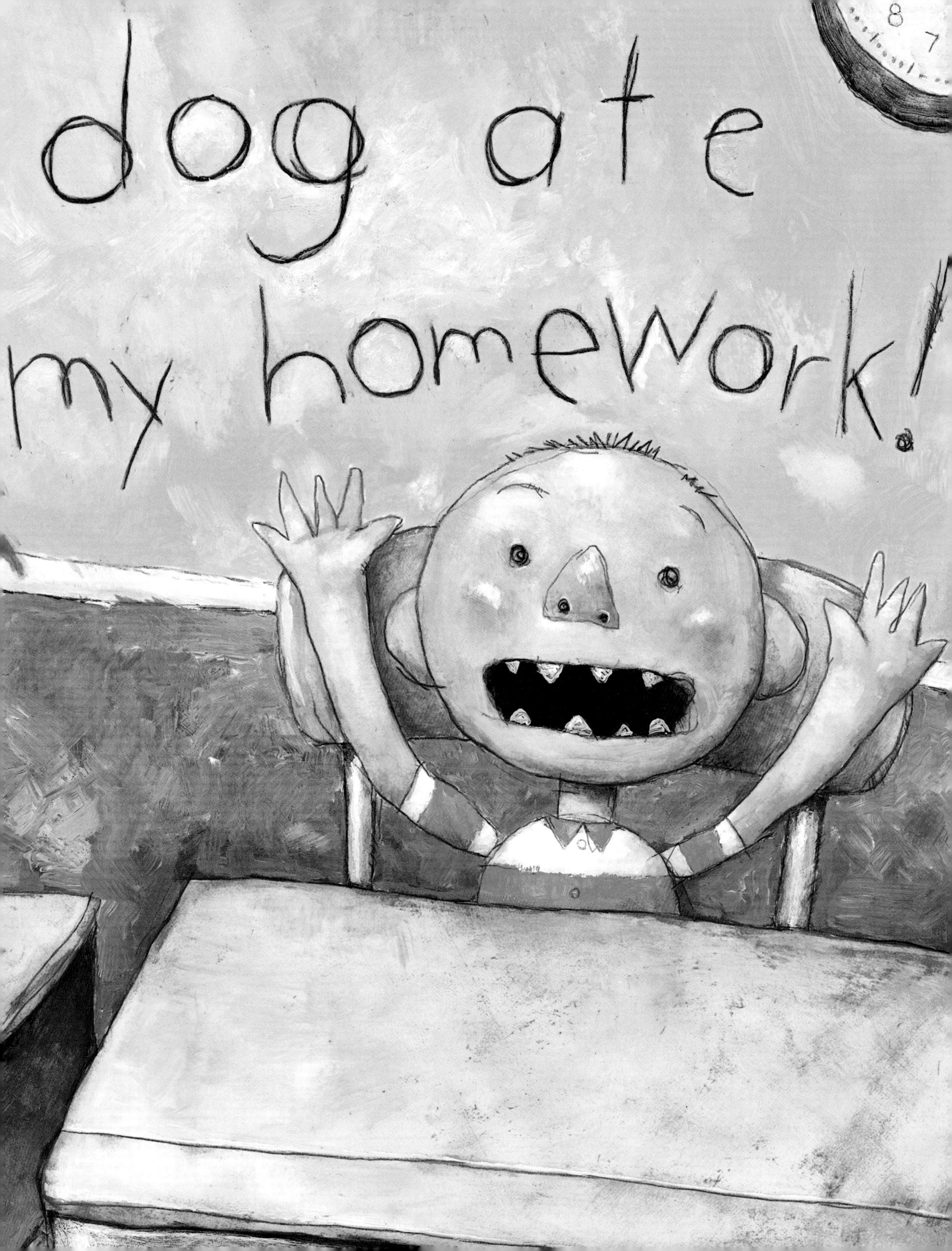
dog ate
my homework!

I couldn't help

DICKENS ELEM

Excuse me!

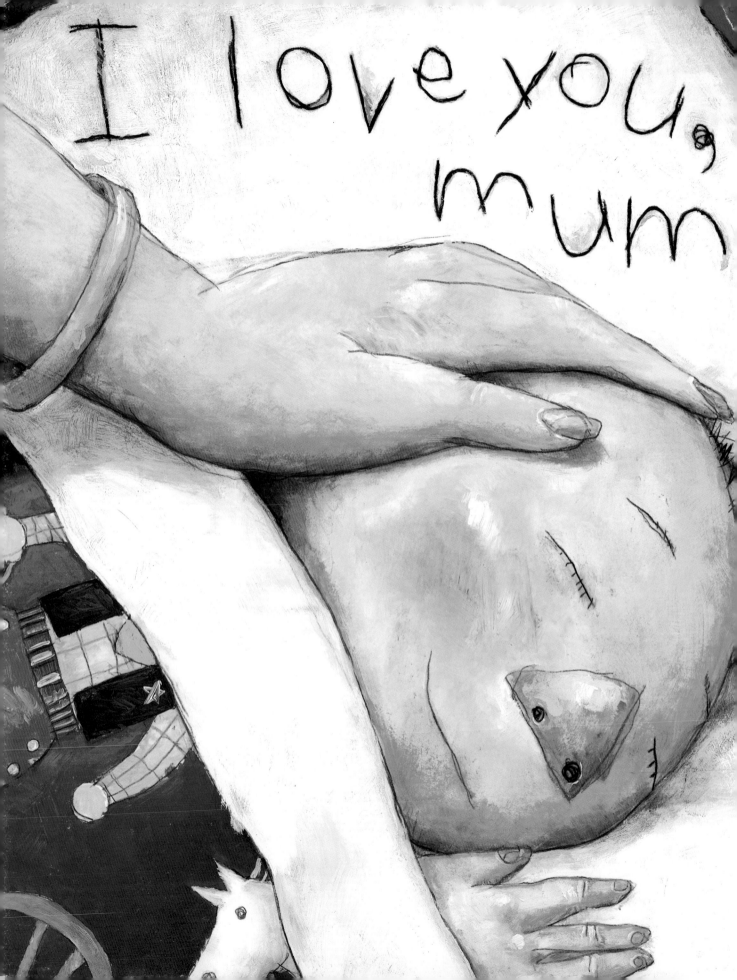